Liza turned to cross the street again. She froze.

About half a block back, on the other side, she saw the girls from Mrs. Lane's class. They were coming this way. They were talking and laughing. Liza didn't think they had seen her yet.

"Come on, Bridget." Liza wanted to get far ahead of the other girls. She turned to pull on Bridget's hand.

But Bridget wasn't there. She had caught up with William again.

"Let's go," said Liza quickly.

"Why?" said Bridget. "What's the hurry?"

Liza couldn't tell her. How could she say that she wanted to get away before her friends from Mrs. Lane's class saw her with Bridget and William? That would be a terrible thing to say to someone.

It was too late anyway.

"Hello, E-liz-a-beth," called a voice from across the street. It was followed by a burst of giggles.

OTHER CHAPTER BOOKS FROM PUFFIN

The William Problem

· Barbara Baker ·

THE William Problem

ILLUSTRATED BY Ann Iosa

PUFFIN BOOKS

PUFFIN BOOKS
Published by the Penguin Group
Penguin Putnam Inc., 375 Hudson Street, New York, New York 10014, U.S.A.
Penguin Books Ltd, 27 Wrights Lane, London W8 5TZ, England
Penguin Books Australia Ltd, Ringwood, Victoria, Australia
Penguin Books Canada Ltd, 10 Alcorn Avenue, Toronto, Ontario, Canada M4V 3B2
Penguin Books (N.Z.) Ltd, 182-190 Wairau Road, Auckland 10, New Zealand

Penguin Books Ltd, Registered Offices: Harmondsworth, Middlesex, England

First published in the United States of America by Dutton Children's Books,
a division of Penguin Books USA Inc., 1994
Published in Puffin Books, 1997

10 9 8 7 6 5 4 3 2

THE LIBRARY OF CONGRESS HAS CATALOGED THE DUTTON EDITION AS FOLLOWS:
Baker, Barbara.
The William problem / by Barbara Baker; illustrated by Ann Iosa.—1st ed. p. cm.
Summary: Liza hates third grade because she is separated from her best friend and
she has mean Mrs. Rumford as her teacher, until she begins to make new friends.
ISBN 0-525-45235-4
[1. Schools—Fiction. 2. Friendship—Fiction.] I. Iosa, Ann, ill. II. Title.
PZ7.B16922Wi 1994 [Fic]—dc20 93-32598 CIP AC

Puffin Books ISBN 0-14-037699-2

Printed in the United States of America

RL: 1.9

FOR MARGARET GABEL

B.A.B.

■ ■ ■

TO DANIELLE AND MICHAEL

A.I.

The William Problem

One

It was Friday morning—at last.

Liza Farmer kicked a pebble along the sidewalk in front of her. "I hate school," she said. "I hate third grade. I wish it was over."

Liza and her best friend, Heather, were walking to school.

Heather's long hair swung back and forth as she walked. "School's not going to be over for a long, long time," she said. "It's only the end of the first week. And anyway, I *love* third grade."

Liza gave the pebble an angry kick. It flew out into the street. She walked faster.

Heather had to run to catch up. "Wait for me," she said. "It's not my fault."

Liza slowed down. Heather was right. It wasn't Heather's fault that everything was going wrong for Liza this year.

Last year Liza and Heather had been in the same class. They did everything together. They were best friends in school, and out of school, too. It was great.

But this year was different.

Heather was lucky. She was in Mrs. Lane's class. Mrs. Lane was pretty, *and* she was nice.

Liza was not lucky. She was in Mrs. Rumford's class. And Mrs. Rumford was the meanest teacher in the whole school. Everybody knew it. Especially Liza. Her big brother, Edward, had had Mrs. Rumford when he was in third grade. He said she was mean. He said third grade was terrible.

Liza sighed. She looked at Heather walking along beside her. Heather was wearing a new red dress. She had red barrettes in her long hair. Today, after school, Heather was going to Monica Marks's birthday party.

Liza was not going. Monica had invited only the girls from Mrs. Lane's class.

Liza sighed again. "I like your dress," she said. "It's pretty."

Heather smiled. "My mother got it for me for the party. I really wish you were coming, too."

"Not me," said Liza. "I wouldn't go to Monica's dumb party if you paid me a million dollars. And anyway, I'm going to Bridget Duffy's house, remember?"

Bridget was a new girl in school. She was in Liza's class. "Remember?" Liza said to Heather again.

Heather nodded. But she didn't say anything. They were coming to the schoolyard. She was looking all around. "There's Monica," she cried. "See you later."

"Wait," said Liza.

But Heather ran off.

Liza followed her through the gate. There were kids everywhere. But Liza was all alone.

Two

The schoolyard was getting crowded. Liza stood near the gate, looking for Bridget. She couldn't find her.

The girls from Mrs. Lane's class were in one corner. They all had party clothes on. Liza looked down at herself. She was wearing her blue jeans and a summer T-shirt. The shirt still smelled a little bit like suntan lotion. She still had her summer haircut, too—short. It looked terrible.

Two girls from Mrs. Rumford's class came through the gate—Nancy Higgins and Amy Cutter. Nancy smiled at Liza. "Hi," she said.

But Amy didn't smile. Amy was stuck-up. She pulled Nancy into the yard after her.

Liza felt as if everyone was looking at her, standing by herself. She had to move. Some older kids were playing double-dutch jump rope on the other side of the yard. Liza made her way over to them. Then she stood there watching. She tried to look very interested.

Finally a whistle blew three times. "Line up," called the principal. She blew the whistle again.

Liza ran over to Mrs. Rumford's line. Everybody was choosing a partner. Amy Cutter and Nancy Higgins, James Rich and Michael Green, Sara Port and Kim Lee . . . Soon everyone was in line with someone—everyone but Liza. Bridget Duffy wasn't there.

Liza looked at the end of the line. Only one person was left without a partner. William Spear.

William Spear was the biggest creep in the whole third grade. Maybe even the whole school. He was skinny. He was as skinny as a spear. And he always had a runny nose. Liza couldn't be William's partner. She just couldn't.

"Elizabeth."

Liza blinked. It was Mrs. Rumford. She always called her Elizabeth—not Liza. Mrs. Rumford wouldn't use nicknames.

"Elizabeth Farmer, we are waiting for you."

Everybody turned to stare at Liza. She stood there for a moment. Then she walked stiffly over to William.

The line started to move. Liza heard pounding footsteps coming up behind her. She turned around. Bridget!

Bridget was wearing her old jeans and a pink T-shirt. Both of her sneaker laces were untied. Her short hair was sticking out.

Liza had never, ever been so happy to see someone. "You're late," she cried. "I thought you weren't coming."

Bridget was panting. "I didn't wake up on time," she said. "I had to run."

Mrs. Rumford stopped. "No talking," she called.

Liza turned around quickly. She wished that

William and Bridget could change places. But it was too late.

William sneezed—a juicy one. Liza wiped her arm. She hoped no one noticed.

The line moved on. The sixth graders were waiting for the younger kids to pass. Liza saw her brother, Edward. He was looking at her—and William Spear.

Edward made a kissy face. He pretended to throw up.

Liza stuck her tongue out at him. Then her class went through the doors into school.

Bridget poked Liza. "Your brother is a pain," she whispered. "But he's kind of cute."

Now *Liza* pretended to throw up.

Mrs. Rumford turned around. The line stopped. "What's going on back there?" she said. "I don't want to hear any more noise from this class. Not one more sound." She stared at everyone for a moment.

It was very quiet. Mrs. Rumford turned back again.

Suddenly William Spear sneezed. It sounded

like a huge explosion in the quiet hall.

Liza jumped. Then she giggled. She couldn't help it. And she couldn't stop. She put her hand over her mouth. A snort came out.

Mrs. Rumford was coming toward her. "What is the meaning of this, young lady?"

Liza stopped laughing. She was really in trouble now.

Mrs. Rumford was waiting.

"I'm sorry," Liza said. "I won't do it again."

"I should say not," said Mrs. Rumford. "Come with me." She led Liza to the front of the line.

Liza had to walk next to Mrs. Rumford all the way to the classroom.

Three

Liza stood out in the hall with Mrs. Rumford. Everyone else was in the classroom.

"This is no way to begin a Friday, Elizabeth," said Mrs. Rumford. "Are you ready to behave yourself?"

Liza looked at the toes of her sneakers. "Yes," she said in a low voice.

"Speak up," said Mrs. Rumford. "Don't mumble."

"Yes," said Liza, a little louder.

"You may go to your seat. But don't let this happen again." Mrs. Rumford went into the room.

Liza followed her. Everybody stared. Liza wanted to turn around and run right out. She would keep running until she was far away from this terrible school. She would never come back.

"We should all be getting ready to work," said Mrs. Rumford to the class.

Liza walked quickly to her desk at the back of the room. She slid into her seat. William Spear's desk was next to hers. He was blowing his nose. She didn't look at him. Bridget was on her other side. She was biting her fingernails. Liza leaned over and whispered, "I told you she was the meanest teacher in the school."

Amy Cutter sat right in front of Liza. She turned around and put her finger to her lips. *"Shhhhh."* She did it as loudly as she could. Liza knew it was for the teacher to hear. Amy was that kind of kid—a big tattletale.

Mrs. Rumford was sitting at her desk. She looked up.

Oh, no, thought Liza. Now I'm really going to get it.

"That will be enough, girls," said Mrs. Rumford. "Settle down."

"But, Mrs. Rumford," said Amy.

"I said that will be enough—both of you."

Liza couldn't believe Mrs. Rumford had said that. Amy Cutter was teacher's pet. Mrs. Rumford *loved* Amy.

Liza looked at Bridget and shrugged her shoulders.

Bridget shrugged back. They smiled at each other.

Liza made a face at Amy's back. Then she took her notebook and a pencil out of her desk. Mrs. Rumford always began the day with board work. Today the board was covered with math problems—adding and taking away. Liza started to copy them. They were easy. But boring.

Soon the only sounds in the room were pencils scratching and William sniffing. Liza wondered what the kids in Mrs. Lane's class were doing. Probably something fun, like planning a trip . . . or maybe doing a science experiment.

A chair scraped across the floor. Mrs. Rum-

ford stood up. "Please get your homework out," she said. Then she walked to the back of the room and sat down at the reading table behind Liza. "Row one," she called.

The kids in the first row stood up and walked back to the reading table. Then they waited in line. Mrs. Rumford checked their homework, one at a time.

Liza was glad she had finished all of hers. It would be torture to stand there without it, just waiting for Mrs. Rumford to find out.

"Row two," called Mrs. Rumford. "And everyone else should be working."

Liza did another problem. Then she took her homework out of her backpack. It was spelling words in sentences and two math worksheets. Liza had also read for an hour in her yellow reader. She had a lot more homework than Heather.

"Row three," called Mrs. Rumford.

William Spear got up. Liza's row would be next. Then Bridget's. That was the last row. Then they would go over the board work.

The dumb, boring board work. Liza wasn't even half finished. She was still doing the adding problems. She looked over at Bridget's paper. She was already doing the takeaways. Bridget was smart.

The kids from row three were coming back to their seats. All except for William Spear.

Liza turned around. William was standing next to Mrs. Rumford. His face was red.

" . . . and I want to see it first thing Monday morning," said Mrs. Rumford, "signed by your mother."

William hurried back to his seat. His head was down. His hands were empty. He must not have done his homework, thought Liza.

"Row four," called Mrs. Rumford.

Liza gathered up her homework. But before she stood up, she took another quick look at William.

William was crying.

Four

Liza was waiting for Mrs. Rumford to check her homework. In her mind, she saw William crying. She didn't want to. She didn't want to think about William at all. But she couldn't help it. He looked so sad, it made Liza feel like crying, too.

But it's his own fault, Liza told herself. He should have done his homework. Everyone else had.

"Elizabeth," said Mrs. Rumford.

Liza stepped up to the table. She put her homework down.

Mrs. Rumford checked it quickly. "This could

be neater," she said. Then she put a check mark on each page.

Liza went back to her desk and slid into her seat. She still had a ton of board work to do. But first she peeked at William. He wasn't crying anymore. Good, she thought. Now she could forget about him. She had to get back to work.

Liza picked up her pencil and did two more problems. She put the pencil down again. She wondered how the other kids were doing. Bridget was still getting her homework checked. Liza looked over at her paper. Finished! Bridget had done every single problem.

Liza looked at William's desk, but she couldn't see his paper. His arm was in the way. She leaned over a little farther.

"Eyes on your own work," called Mrs. Rumford.

Liza jumped. She looked down at her paper. Now Mrs. Rumford probably thought she was cheating.

Liza wished school was finished. She wished she was on her way to Bridget's house. She wished that Monica's party was over, and that it was a terrible party, and that Heather hated it. Liza shook her head a little. Ha! she said to herself. It was probably going to be a great party. Heather would love it.

Bridget sat down at her desk. Liza looked over at her. Bridget's shoelaces were tied now. But her clothes were a mess, and her hair was even shorter than Liza's.

Bridget looked up and grinned.

Liza smiled back a little. Bridget was nice, and she was smart. But she just wasn't Heather.

Mrs. Rumford stood up and walked to the front of the room. "I hope you have all been working hard," she said. "Who would like to show us how to do the first example on the board?"

Liza had *not* been working hard. She wasn't finished. But she was sure that her first answer was right. She raised her hand. If she did one on the board now, Mrs. Rumford wouldn't pick her later.

"Amy," said Mrs. Rumford. "You may come up."

Amy walked to the board. She wrote her answer neatly.

"Good," said Mrs. Rumford. "Did everyone get the same answer as Amy?"

Bro-ther, thought Liza. Who would be dumb enough to say no?

They went on to the next problem. Then the next. Liza kept raising her hand. Mrs. Rumford kept calling on others.

Liza was getting nervous. Finally they were up to the last problem that she had finished. It was easy. A baby could add those numbers. Liza raised her hand and waved it around as hard as she could.

"Elizabeth," called Mrs. Rumford.

Liza hurried up to the board. She wrote her answer quickly.

"Did everyone get the same answer as Elizabeth?" said Mrs. Rumford.

Liza started back toward her seat.

"*Just* a minute," said Mrs. Rumford. "I don't

think everyone *did* get the same answer, Elizabeth."

Liza stopped. Joseph Russo was raising his hand. Joseph was the smartest kid in the class in math. When the other kids saw Joseph, they put their hands up, too.

"Please put your hands down," said Mrs. Rumford. "Let's let Elizabeth correct her work by herself."

Liza went back to the board. She erased her answer. Then she stood there. She couldn't think, not with everyone staring at her like that. She picked up the chalk.

"Put that down, Elizabeth. I want you to *think* first. Now look at the problem carefully."

Liza stared at the board.

"Elizabeth," said Mrs. Rumford. "What is this problem telling you to do?"

"Um . . . to add the bottom number to the top number?" said Liza.

Mrs. Rumford frowned.

"I mean, the top number to the bottom." One of them had to be right.

"Look *again,* more carefully," said Mrs. Rumford.

Liza did, and then she saw it. There was a takeaway sign, as clear as anything. It wasn't an adding problem at all. "Oh," she said. "It's takeaway."

"Subtraction," said Mrs. Rumford. "Can you do it now?"

"Yes," said Liza. She picked up the chalk. It was not such an easy problem, though. Liza had to count on her fingers. She tried to do it without moving them. Mrs. Rumford said all third graders should know their number facts.

Finally Liza had the answer.

"That's correct," said Mrs. Rumford. "You need to work more carefully, Elizabeth. And you need to learn your number facts. Third graders don't use their fingers for counting."

Liza hurried back to her seat.

"Ha ha," Amy whispered as Liza passed.

Liza wanted to reach out and give her hair a good pull. But she didn't. Amy would tell.

Nothing went right the rest of the day. Even lunch was spoiled. Liza sat next to Bridget, and that was good. But William Spear sat right across from them. He didn't say anything. He never did. He just sat there eating and sniffing—yuck!

And Liza could see Heather and the other kids from Mrs. Lane's class on the far side of the lunchroom. She waved to Heather, but Heather didn't wave back. Liza worried about it all afternoon.

Finally it was almost time to go home. Everyone was ready.

"Homework," said Mrs. Rumford. "I almost forgot."

The class groaned.

"I'm waiting." Mrs. Rumford crossed her arms.

The class got quiet.

"That's better." Mrs. Rumford looked around the room. "I want you all to go over your number facts this weekend. We cannot learn to multiply until we can add and subtract without using our fingers. There will be a test Monday morning."

Everyone groaned again. Amy Cutter turned around. "It's your fault, stupid," she hissed at Liza.

Some of the other kids were giving Liza dirty looks, too.

"Line up," said Mrs. Rumford. "Row one first."

Liza waited for Bridget. They got in line together.

"Have a nice weekend," said Mrs. Rumford.

The class filed out into the hall and down the stairs.

"I'm glad you're coming to my house," said Bridget.

"Me, too," said Liza. But it felt strange not to be walking home with Heather. Liza and Heather lived on the same street. They *always* walked home together. But not today.

Five

Let's go," said Liza. She and Bridget were outside the school. Kids were still coming through the doors.

"Wait a minute," said Bridget. "I've got to tie my shoelaces." They were both undone again. She knelt down.

Liza groaned. She wanted to get away before Mrs. Lane's class came out. She didn't want to see Heather with Monica and those other girls. "Come *on*," she said to Bridget.

"I'm ready." Bridget stood up. They started to walk. Bridget lived the opposite way from Liza. "What do you want to do at my house?"

she said. "I've got checkers and some other games. Or we could draw or do something else if you want to."

"It doesn't matter to me," said Liza. What she really wanted to do was see Bridget's room. She wanted to see how it looked and what kinds of things she had. But she couldn't say that. Bridget might think she was nosy.

They walked along quietly for a moment.

Liza was thinking about school, about Mrs. Rumford. "You know what?" she said. "I saw William crying in school today."

"You did?" said Bridget. "When? I didn't see him cry."

"I think I was the only one. It was when Mrs. Rumford was checking the homework. William didn't have it. She said he has to bring it in on Monday. And his mother has to sign it." Liza remembered how sad William had looked.

"That's weird," said Bridget. "I wonder why he didn't do his homework. He never comes out to play after school."

Liza was surprised. "How do you know?"

"He lives next door to me," said Bridget. "And he only goes out in his backyard. I think his mother is very strict."

"Oh." Somehow Liza couldn't imagine William living next door to someone. She was glad he didn't live near her.

"Look," said Bridget. She pointed across the street. "There's William. Let's ask him."

"I don't want . . . ," Liza started.

But Bridget was already crossing the street. "Hey, William," she yelled.

Liza took a few steps after her. She didn't want to talk to William. She didn't want to see him. She didn't even want to know that there *was* a William Spear. But Bridget was going over to talk to him, and Liza had to follow.

William stopped when Bridget called his name. But he didn't look happy about it.

"Why didn't you do your homework?" said Bridget. "Liza said—"

William's face got red. "I *did* do it." He started to walk away.

"Forget it," Liza said to Bridget. "Let's just go." She turned to cross the street again.

She froze.

About half a block back, on the other side, she saw the girls from Mrs. Lane's class. They were coming this way. They were talking and laughing. Liza didn't think they had seen her yet.

"Come on, Bridget." Liza wanted to get far ahead of the other girls. She turned to pull on Bridget's hand.

But Bridget wasn't there. She had caught up with William again.

Liza ran after them. She grabbed Bridget's arm. "Let's go," she said. "Come on."

"Wait a minute," said Bridget. "William *did* do his homework. But he forgot to bring it. Right, William?"

William nodded miserably. He sniffed.

Bridget went on. "And Mrs. Rumford said forgetting is no excuse. I don't think that's fair."

"I don't either," said Liza quickly. "Let's go."

"Why?" said Bridget. "What's the hurry?"

Liza couldn't tell her. How could she say that she wanted to get away before her friends from Mrs. Lane's class saw her with Bridget and William? That would be a terrible thing to say to someone.

It was too late anyway.

"Hello, E-liz-a-beth," called a voice from across the street. It was followed by a burst of giggles.

Liza felt her face getting red. She didn't turn around. Maybe if she didn't look, they would think she was someone else. Maybe they would just keep going.

"That girl is calling you," said Bridget.

"I know." Liza still didn't turn around.

Bridget looked confused.

"It's Monica Marks," William told her. "She's mean."

Liza looked at William. Bridget didn't know what was going on. But *he* did.

"They're leaving now," said William quietly.

Liza shrugged her shoulders as if she didn't care.

"What's the matter?" said Bridget.

"Nothing. It's not important." Liza turned to watch the girls walking away. She saw them stop at a big house on the corner. "Is that where Monica lives?" she asked William. Liza didn't know this neighborhood well at all.

William nodded.

Monica and the other girls ran up the steps and into the house. The last one was Heather. She turned back and waved at Liza. Then Heather, in her bright red dress, disappeared into the house. The door closed behind her.

"I guess we'd better go," said Liza. They started to walk slowly.

William walked a little apart.

"Liza," said Bridget. "The girl with the red dress is a friend of yours, isn't she?"

Liza felt a hot lump in her throat. "I guess so," she said. "She lives near me." Maybe Heather didn't want to be her best friend anymore. Maybe she just wanted to be Monica's friend now.

They passed Monica's house on the other side of the street. Liza didn't look.

Six

Liza didn't want to go to Bridget's house anymore. She wanted to turn around and go home. But she couldn't. That would hurt Bridget's feelings. So she kept walking.

Finally they came to a small brick house.

"Good-bye," mumbled William. He started to climb the front steps.

"Hey, William," said Bridget. "You want to come to my house for a while? Liza's coming."

William turned back. He looked surprised and happy and sad all at the same time. Liza thought he was going to say yes. That would ruin everything.

"No, thank you," said William quickly. Then he ran up the rest of the steps, opened his door, and vanished inside. The door slammed behind him.

"That was close," said Liza. "Why did you ask him to come, anyway? He's such a creep."

"I told you," said Bridget. "I knew he wouldn't do it. He never comes out front after school."

"Oh, right," said Liza. But she wished Bridget would be more careful. What if William had said *yes?* Liza would just die if she had to spend the afternoon with William Spear.

The next house was Bridget's. She led the way up the stairs. "It's a big mess inside," she said. "We're not finished unpacking yet."

"I don't care," said Liza. She knew that Bridget had just moved here during the summer.

But when they went inside, she was surprised. It really *was* a big mess. Boxes were all over the place. Some were closed. Some were open, with things spilling out.

"Mom," yelled Bridget. "I'm home."

"In here," called a voice.

Liza followed Bridget down the hall to the kitchen.

Mrs. Duffy was sitting at the table. "I'm just taking a coffee break," she said. She took a sip from a blue mug. Then she stood up. She was dressed almost the same as Bridget. But her jeans and T-shirt were splotched with paint.

"This is Liza," said Bridget.

Mrs. Duffy smiled. "Nice to meet you, Liza. I'll be in my studio, Bridget, if you need me." She walked slowly out of the kitchen, taking her coffee mug with her.

"She means the living room," said Bridget. "That's where she paints, so she calls it her studio."

"What?" said Liza.

"My mother is an artist. She has her easel set up in the living room. Nobody is supposed to go in there."

"Not even your *father?*" said Liza.

Bridget turned away. "He doesn't live here. They're divorced."

"Oh." Liza couldn't think of anything else

to say. Everything was so different at Bridget's house. Not like Liza's at all.

"Are you hungry?" said Bridget after a moment. She opened the refrigerator and pulled out a carton of milk. Then she took two dirty glasses from the sink and rinsed them. "I know we have some cookies somewhere," she said. She started to look through the cabinets.

Liza stood by the door, watching. She hated milk, but she didn't say a word.

Finally Bridget found a box of cookies. "Let's go up to my room," she said. "Here, you can carry the glasses."

Liza followed Bridget out of the kitchen and down the hall. She had to walk carefully so she wouldn't trip over boxes and piles of things scattered around.

They stopped in front of a closed door. "We're going upstairs," Bridget yelled.

"Okay," her mother called back.

"Come on," said Bridget. She led the way. Upstairs they passed two doors. Then she stopped and pushed open the third door. "*My* room."

Seven

Liza followed Bridget into her bedroom. She put the glasses down and dropped her backpack. Then she looked around.

It was a great room. The walls were pale yellow, and along one wall Bridget had shelves filled with games and art supplies and books —millions of books. There was a big globe on the top shelf and a collection of dolls from around the world. They were beautiful. And Bridget had a rocking chair and a desk with little cubbyholes.

Liza wished she could have a real desk and a rocking chair. She wished she could have a room of her own. She had to share her bedroom with her little sister, Peggy.

She wondered why Bridget's room was so neat, not messy like the rest of the house, or like Bridget herself. She couldn't ask, though. "I love your room, Bridget," she said.

Bridget was looking out her open window. "Come here," she said. "I want to show you something."

Liza went over to the window.

Bridget pointed. "That's William's backyard. He'll probably come out soon."

William's yard was small, but there was a picnic table with benches. "What does he do out there?" Liza asked.

"I don't know. You want to look later?"

"Okay," said Liza. "But I don't want him to see me."

Bridget grinned. "We can pretend that we're spying," she said. "He won't see a thing."

"Good," said Liza. She grinned back.

Bridget sat down on the floor. "Let's eat now. I'm starving."

"I'm hungry, too," said Liza. "But can we play one of your games while we're eating?"

"Okay," said Bridget. "You pick one." She started to pour the milk.

Liza chose Parcheesi. Heather had that game, too. It was fun to play.

When the game was set up on the floor, Liza took a cookie. She bit into it. It was as hard as cement.

"They're a little stale," said Bridget. "But they're good with milk."

Liza nodded. She took a gulp of milk and swished it around in her mouth with the cookie. She swallowed. She could feel it going down her throat—kind of heavy and scratchy. "I'm not really very hungry," she said. "Maybe later." She pushed her snack aside.

They started to play. Liza was thinking about school again. "Everybody's mad at me," she said. "Because of the math homework."

Bridget rolled the dice. "I'm not mad at you."

"Well, everybody else blames me. And it's not fair. It's Mrs. Rumford's fault. She's so mean."

Bridget jumped up. "I think I heard a door,"

she said. She looked out the window. "I did. It's William."

Liza scrambled up and stood next to Bridget. "Move back a little. He might see us."

William had a pile of things. A big box of tissues was on top. He put everything on the picnic table. Then he sat down. His back was to them.

"Rats!" said Liza. "We can't see what he's doing."

They heard a sound.

Liza giggled. "Blowing his nose—that's what he's doing."

William turned around. He looked up. Bridget and Liza ducked. They put their hands over their mouths so William wouldn't hear them laughing.

After a minute, Bridget said, "What should we do now? We can't see what he's doing from up here."

They sat on the floor, thinking.

"I have an idea," said Liza. "Let's take our things out to your backyard. We can see him better from there."

"Forget it," said Bridget. "Didn't you see what a mess it is? It's full of weeds and old junk."

"It's not that bad," Liza lied. "Come on. Don't be a chicken."

"Who's a chicken?" Bridget scooped up the Parcheesi game. She pulled the blanket off her bed. "We'll need this to sit on. You bring the milk and cookies."

When they got to the back door, Liza said, "Maybe we shouldn't."

Bridget gave her a look. "Now who's the chicken?" Then she pushed the door open and went out.

"Hey, wait for me," cried Liza. "I was just kidding."

There was a low fence between Bridget's yard and William's. William looked over when he heard them.

"Hi, William," Bridget called.

"Hi," William answered. Then he turned away.

"Want to play Parcheesi with us?" Bridget tried again.

Liza poked her in the side and made a

face. She wanted to spy on William, not play with him.

"No," said William. "I'm busy."

Liza breathed a sigh of relief.

Bridget spread her blanket out. Liza helped her set up the Parcheesi game. "Well, I guess we'll just have to play by ourselves," Bridget said, loud enough for William to hear.

They played until Liza won. Then they started all over again. "This is stupid," Liza whispered. "We can't see a thing he's doing. *Some* spies."

"I know," said Bridget. "But I've got an idea. Watch this." She stood up and walked to the fence. She started to climb over it.

William heard her coming. "Hey, you can't—"

"Yes, we can," said Bridget. "We're just visiting. Come on, Liza."

Liza climbed the fence after Bridget. They walked over to the picnic table.

William quickly hid something under his pile of papers.

"What are you doing, William?" said Bridget. She sat down opposite him.

"Just homework. I'm practicing number facts."

"William," said Bridget. "It's only Friday. Why are you doing homework now? Why can't you come over and play one little game of Parcheesi?"

Liza rolled her eyes.

"Maybe I just don't want to," said William. He covered the pile of papers with his arms.

They weren't getting anywhere. Liza wanted to leave, go back inside, and look at Bridget's dolls or books or something. But she was curious. What had William hidden under those papers? She was pretty sure it wasn't just his homework.

Suddenly William sneezed. He reached for a tissue.

At the same time, Liza reached out and grabbed the pile of papers.

"Hey, give me that!" William jumped up.

"Come and get it," said Liza. She ran over to the fence.

Bridget caught up with her first.

William ran after them. "Give me my papers!" he yelled.

Liza scrambled over the fence. Bridget was right behind her. They turned around.

William was coming after them. And he looked angry. Angry enough to explode.

"Inside!" Bridget yelled to Liza. Then they ran. Bridget's back door slammed behind them. They pounded down the hall and up the stairs. They didn't stop running until they reached Bridget's room.

Liza threw herself down on the floor. She was still holding William's papers.

Eight

Bridget walked over to her window and looked out. "Nobody there," she said. "I guess he went home." She dropped down next to Liza. "Why did you take his homework?" She frowned a little.

Liza stared at the papers in her hand. "I didn't mean to keep it," she said. "I was just fooling around. Honest. I didn't think he'd get so mad."

"All right," said Bridget. "I believe you. But what are you going to do now?"

"Do?" said Liza. "What do you mean?"

Bridget pointed at the papers. "You know. If

you're not going to keep them, maybe you should take them back."

"*I'm* not going over there," said Liza. "No way! Didn't you see how mad he was? He probably went right in and told his mother on us." She flipped through William's papers. Suddenly she stopped. "Bridget, look at this!" She held a page out.

"Oh!" said Bridget. "So that's what he was hiding."

They looked through William's papers together. The one on the top was filled with math problems. But the papers underneath were different. They were all drawings by William—of people in their class. And they were *not* nice.

"Look at this one," said Liza. She pointed. It was a picture of a mean-looking woman. At the bottom of the page, it said *Mrs. Dumford.*

"*Dumb.* That's pretty funny," said Bridget. "Mrs. *Dumb*ford."

Liza tried to hide the next paper under the stack.

Bridget grabbed it. *"Bridget the Brain,"* she read out loud. She looked at the picture of herself. It showed a girl with short, messy hair. The girl's shoelaces were flopping. She had her fingers in her mouth.

Bridget quickly pulled her hand away from her own mouth. "I guess I do chew my nails too much," she said. "Let's see if he did one of you."

Liza hoped that he hadn't. She flipped through the rest of the pictures. "No," she said. "He didn't get to me yet. But look. He did one of himself." She held it out.

"Bill Spear," Bridget read. "I didn't know William was called Bill."

"He's not," said Liza. "I mean, I never heard anyone call him Bill in school."

They looked at the drawing. It was a picture of a boy with huge muscles in his arms and a wide smile on his face.

"Sure doesn't look like William," said Liza. "I know what's missing."

"What?" said Bridget.

"Wait a minute. I'll show you." Liza jumped up. She went over to the desk and found a pencil. Then she drew something on William's

face. "There," she said. "Now it looks like him. He just needed a runny nose."

"Yuck," said Bridget. She giggled. "Here, give me the pencil."

Liza passed it over. She was giggling, too.

Bridget drew something in William's hand. "I gave him a tissue," she said. Then she wrote *William the drip, drip, drip* on the bottom of the paper.

They both cracked up.

"We'd better erase it now," said Liza.

Suddenly the phone rang downstairs. *"Bridget . . . Li-za,"* called Mrs. Duffy.

"Oh, no!" cried Liza. "What if it's William's mother? What if he told on us?"

"Li-za," Bridget's mother called again. "Your mother wants you to come home now."

"Okay," Liza yelled back. She looked at Bridget. "That was close," she said. "I thought we were in big trouble."

"Me, too," said Bridget. "But you know what? I don't think he's going to tell."

"Why?" said Liza. "I would if I was him."

Bridget shrugged. "I just don't think he will. I don't think he's such a bad kid. I feel sorry for him."

Liza didn't say anything for a moment. She was thinking about William and his pictures. She wished she hadn't taken them. It was a mean thing to do.

She stood up. "I guess I'd better go home now," she said. She got her backpack. Then she gathered William's papers into a neat pile. They didn't seem very funny anymore—not very funny at all. "Oh, what am I going to do, Bridget? I don't want to keep these until Monday."

"Poor William." Bridget sighed.

"Well, what do you want me to do?" said Liza. "Do you want me to just go over there and ring his doorbell? Do you want me to get killed or something?"

Bridget didn't answer. She just looked at Liza.

Liza stared back. "Well, if you're so brave, why don't *you* do it?"

Bridget shook her head. "*I* didn't take his papers. And anyway, I didn't *say* you should give them back."

"But I *have* to," Liza cried. And suddenly she knew it was the truth. She was the one who had teased William and grabbed his papers away. And she was the one who had to give them back.

"Do you want me to go with you?" said Bridget in a small voice. "I will if you really want me to."

"No," said Liza. "It's okay. I can do it by myself."

Nine

Liza stood in front of Bridget's house. She held William's papers in a tight grip. She took a deep breath. Then she started to walk. Too bad William's house was only next door. Too bad it wasn't far away—like about a million miles.

Don't be a baby, Liza told herself. She walked slowly to the foot of William's steps. Then, before she could change her mind, she ran up the steps and rang the bell.

William answered the door.

Liza held the papers out in front of her. "I'm sorry," she mumbled. "I didn't mean to really take them."

William grabbed his papers. "Did you look at them?"

"No," said Liza. She could feel her face getting hot.

William didn't look as if he believed her. He started to close the door.

"Wait," said Liza.

William stopped.

"Did you . . . did you tell your mother?"

"No." William shook his head. "I didn't."

"Good," said Liza. "I mean, thank you . . . and, um . . ."

"William," called his mother, "who's at the door? Tell them I'll be there in just a minute."

Liza didn't want to meet Mrs. Spear. She started backing down the stairs.

William closed the door.

Liza turned and ran. She ran until she was out of sight of William's house. I did it, she thought. I really did it. She slowed down. It was a relief to be rid of those papers. She didn't like William, but she didn't want to be mean to him. She didn't like being mean to anyone.

Liza walked along, swinging her backpack. She had a lot to think about. Bridget had asked her to visit again next week. This time they would stay away from William. Liza wanted to get a better look at Bridget's doll collection and her books and art stuff.

And maybe Liza would invite Bridget to come to her house after school one day, too. It would be fun if she could keep Peggy out of the way.

"*Liza,* wait up."

Liza looked around. It was Heather. She was coming out of Monica's house with some other kids. She waved good-bye to them as she ran toward Liza.

Liza smiled. She'd been so busy thinking about Bridget that she'd almost forgotten Heather. She waited for her to catch up. "How was the party?" she asked.

"It was okay," said Heather. "Are you still mad?"

"No," said Liza. "I'm glad I went to Bridget's house. You should see all the things she has. And I'm going again next week."

"That's good," said Heather. "Because I'm going to Monica's house tomorrow. And look what she gave me." Heather held out her arm. She was wearing a brand-new friendship bracelet.

Liza stared at the friendship bracelet. She felt as if Heather had slapped her. Her throat was beginning to burn, and her eyes were stinging. But she wouldn't cry. "It's pretty," she said. Then she turned and walked away as fast as she could.

"Slow down," said Heather. She hurried to catch up.

"Can't." Liza walked faster. She wiped a tear away. It had been a terrible week. And now Heather was going to spend Saturday with Monica. It wasn't fair.

Liza began to run. She didn't stop until she

reached her house. "Bye," she called as she ran up her front steps.

"Wait," said Heather.

Liza stopped. "What?"

Heather was panting. "See you tomorrow. That's all."

"But I thought you were going to Monica's house tomorrow," said Liza. "Didn't you say—"

"Only in the morning," said Heather. "Then I can see you in the afternoon. Okay?"

Liza almost said yes. She really wanted to. But then she remembered the friendship bracelet. "Too bad," she said. "I won't be here."

"Where—" Heather started.

"Shopping," said Liza quickly. "My mother's taking me and Peggy for new shoes." The minute she said it, she was sorry. It was a lie. Her mother wasn't taking her anyplace.

"Oh," said Heather. "Well, I guess I'll stay at Monica's house, then." She didn't seem sad about it at all.

"See if I care," yelled Liza. And she opened her door, ran inside the porch, and slammed the door behind her. She stood there, breathing hard. She could see Heather in her mind saying, *Well, I guess I'll stay at Monica's house, then.* That's probably what she really wanted to do anyway. Some best friend *she* was.

"Liza," her mother called from the kitchen. "Is that you?"

"Yes," Liza yelled back. "I have to go to the bathroom. I'll be there in a minute." She dropped her backpack on the porch floor and ran upstairs. The bathroom door was closed. Liza banged on it.

"Who's there?" yelled Edward.

"Me," said Liza. "Hurry up. I've got to go."

"Tough," said Edward. "You'll just have to hold it."

Liza gave the door another good thump. Then she stomped into her bedroom and threw herself on her bed. "A person can't even go to the bathroom in this dumb house," she muttered.

"Liza," yelled Peggy. She came running into the room.

Liza glared at her. "And a person can't have any privacy either."

Peggy stuck her tongue out. "It's my room, too. And Mommy said you have to set the table."

Liza got off her bed and stomped back to the bathroom.

The door opened. "It's all yours," said Edward grandly.

Liza rushed past him into the bathroom. She locked the door behind her. Then she went over and pushed the window all the way up. She leaned her elbows on the sill.

Liza sighed. This was her special place. It was the only place where she could be alone when she was sad or angry, or when she just wanted to be by herself.

From here she could look out over the backyards up and down her block, spread out like a giant patchwork quilt before her.

Her own yard was bare except for a few

scraggly bushes along the sides and a big old tree in one corner. Chester, her dog, was napping in a patch of sunlight. Liza called to him. His tail thumped a few times, but he didn't get up.

Liza stuck her head out of the window and breathed in deeply. The cool air smelled good. She looked up and down the row of yards. Birds flitted from tree to tree. A breeze ruffled the leftover summer flowers. Liza felt herself begin to relax.

Suddenly there was a loud thump on the bathroom door.

Liza jumped. She hit her head on the window. "Who's there?" she said angrily.

"Me," said Peggy. "Mommy said to tell you there's someone on the phone for you."

Heather, thought Liza. And she opened the door and ran downstairs. She would tell Heather that it was a mistake about the shoes. She would tell her they could see each other tomorrow after all.

Liza snatched up the phone. "Heather?"

"No, it's me, Bridget."

"Oh," said Liza. "Hi."

"We forgot something," said Bridget quickly. "I just remembered. We forgot to erase the marks we made on—"

"Oh, no!" cried Liza. "On William's papers."

Eleven

"Liza," her mother called from the kitchen. "Time to set the table."

Liza was still talking to Bridget. "I've got to get off the phone," she told her. "My mother's calling me again."

"Okay," said Bridget. "I'll see you Monday. Don't forget to study for the math test."

"I won't," said Liza. "Bye." She hung up the phone. She sat there twisting the phone cord around her finger. How could Bridget think about math now? Liza couldn't. She had other things to worry about—much more important than a dumb old math test.

William was going to feel terrible when he saw his marked-up picture. Poor William.

And Heather! Liza wished she hadn't lied about going shopping. She wished she hadn't yelled at Heather and slammed her door.

Everything was going wrong. But what could she do?

"Liza, I'm *not* going to call you again." Her mother sounded angry.

"Coming," said Liza. She dropped the phone cord and hurried out to the kitchen. She had an idea. It would work if she could convince her mother.

Peggy was putting glasses on the table. Edward was letting Chester in from the backyard.

Liza gathered up some silverware. "Mom . . . ," she said.

Her mother was at the stove. "Liza, don't set a place for your father. He's working late. And I wish you wouldn't make me call you ten times to set the table. You know it's your job." She opened the oven door and peered in.

"I'm sorry," said Liza. She counted out the

forks and spoons. "Mom . . . ," she tried again.

Mrs. Farmer took the lid off a pan. "Good," she said. "The liver is done."

Liver. Liza hated liver. It smelled terrible, and it tasted terrible, too. It seemed to grow bigger in your mouth the more you chewed it.

"Mom," said Liza, "can I get new shoes tomorrow?"

"No," said her mother.

"But—"

"Your sneakers are almost brand-new."

"Party shoes," said Liza. "That's what I need."

Mrs. Farmer scooped mashed potatoes into a bowl. "When is the party?" she asked.

"I don't know," said Liza. "I mean, I haven't been invited to one yet."

"Fine," said her mother. "When you are, we'll talk about shoes—not now."

Liza gave up. She was quiet during dinner. She was still thinking about Heather and William. She ate her string beans and a few bites of liver. Then she carefully covered the rest of the liver with her mashed potatoes. She looked up from her plate. Edward was watching.

Liza waited for Edward to tell on her. But he didn't say a word. She wondered why. Soon she saw Edward slip a piece of his own meat under the table. Liza leaned over and took a quick look. Chester was standing there wagging his tail and licking his lips.

Liza sat up. She grinned at Edward. He grinned back.

"Peggy," said their mother, "eat your liver."

Poor kid, thought Liza. That liver was cold and fuzzy-tasting by now.

Liza pushed her chair back. "I'm finished," she said. "Can I go out for a little while?"

"Okay," said her mother. "But don't go far."

"I won't," said Liza. She knew what she was going to do. She was going to go to Heather's house. She'd tell her that they could get together tomorrow. She'd explain the whole thing. Heather would understand. She was a good friend.

Liza hurried outside. She closed the front

door behind her. Heather lived only a few houses away. It would just take a minute to go over there.

Liza started down her steps. Then she stopped. Heather's door was opening. Heather came out and looked around. She was still wearing her party dress.

"Heather," Liza called. She smiled and waved.

Heather looked right at her. But she didn't smile or wave. She turned away.

Liza couldn't believe it. There must be some mistake.

Then Heather's mother and father came out. They all walked down their steps and across the sidewalk. Their car was parked at the curb. They got in.

Liza watched Heather's car pull away. She tried to pretend that she didn't care at all.

Twelve

Liza sat on her front steps. She felt terrible. Heather had been her best friend for a long time. But not anymore. Liza stared at the toes of her almost-new sneakers.

The door opened behind her. "Liza," said Peggy, "can I play with you?"

"I'm not playing." Liza pulled at a little piece of rubber on one sneaker. It snapped back.

Peggy sat down next to her. "Mommy's mad at me because I wouldn't finish my liver. It almost made me throw up."

Liza looked up and down the street. She wished Heather would come back. She could see it in her mind. Heather would get out of her car and come over to Liza. "I'm sorry, Liza," she would say. "I still want to be your best friend." Then she would take Monica's friendship bracelet off and throw it away.

"Will you read to me?" said Peggy.

Liza shook her head no.

"Please," begged Peggy. "Just one little book. A teeny one. Then I won't bother you anymore. I promise."

"Oh, all right," said Liza. "Go get one."

Peggy ran inside.

Liza looked up the street again, but she knew Heather wasn't coming. And she knew that Heather would never throw away that friendship bracelet.

Peggy came back and sat down. She gave her book to Liza. "This is a good one," she said.

Liza began to read. It was a super-boring baby book. She read the whole thing.

"That was a good story," said Peggy. "Wasn't it?"

"Great." Liza closed the book. "But that's enough for now. I'm going in."

"Me, too," said Peggy. She followed Liza into the house. *"Mommy,"* she called. "Will you read to me?"

Liza settled down in front of the television. But she didn't turn it on. She was thinking about Heather. There had to be something she could do.

Edward came in, eating an apple. He looked at Liza. "Good show?" he asked.

"Ha ha ha," said Liza.

Edward turned the TV on. He flipped the channels.

Liza watched him for a moment. Then she had an idea. Edward had lots of friends. Maybe he could help her. "Edward?" she said slowly.

"What?" He sat down on the floor.

"Umm . . . well . . . pretend you had a big fight with your best friend when you were my age, and your best friend didn't want to be your best friend anymore. What would you do?"

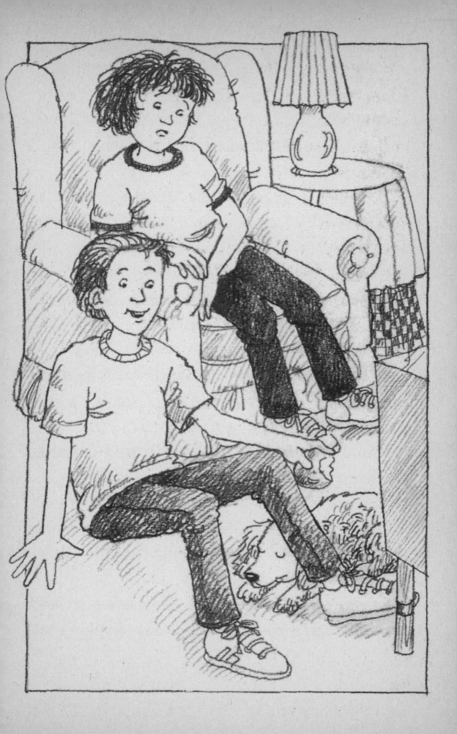

"What happened?" said Edward. "Did you have a fight with your creepy little friend Heather?"

"Of course not," said Liza. "I'm just asking. That's all."

"I'd punch him out," said Edward.

"No, *really*," said Liza. "What would you really do?"

Edward took a big bite of his apple. "I'd just play with someone else," he said. "No big deal. And don't ask me any more questions. I want to watch this show."

Liza thought about what Edward said. It might be no big deal for him. But it wasn't the same for her. Not at all.

"Why don't you call that boy?" said Edward.

"What boy?" Liza asked.

"The skinny kid in your class. The one you were in line with this morning. You could ask him for a date." Edward laughed. "That's a good one."

"Very funny," said Liza. But Edward had given her an idea. Maybe she *should* see someone else tomorrow. Why not? She jumped up and hurried from the room.

Liza dialed Bridget's number carefully.

Bridget answered the phone.

"Hi," said Liza. "I was wondering if we could get together tomorrow. Not wait until Monday."

"I can't," said Bridget. "I promised my mother I'd help her unpack boxes tomorrow."

"I could help you," said Liza. "If you want me to."

"Sure I do," said Bridget. "Let me ask my mother. I'll be right back."

Liza could hear Bridget running off. She hoped her mother would say yes. Unpacking boxes didn't sound like much fun. But staying home by herself would be worse— much worse.

Thirteen

It was Saturday morning.

Liza opened her front door and stepped outside. She was wearing an old pair of shorts and a faded T-shirt. She was all ready to help Bridget unpack boxes.

"Li-za," her mother called from inside, "wait a minute." She came rushing out holding a paper bag. "Here," she said. "Something to share with Bridget."

Liza took the bag and peeked inside. "Mmmmm, oatmeal cookies." They were the soft, chewy kind. Delicious. She remembered Bridget's hard-as-cement cookies. "Thanks, Mom. These are really great."

"Have a good time," said her mother. Then she went back in and closed the door.

Liza stood there for a moment. It was a beautiful day—warm and sunny. Maybe she and Bridget could play outside for a while—after they unpacked some boxes. Then they could have a cookie break.

Liza smiled to herself as she started down her front steps. Today was probably going to be fun.

She had just reached the sidewalk when she heard another door open. She looked up. It was Heather, wearing her newest shorts and a matching top. Liza got a sick feeling in her stomach.

Heather saw her right away. She froze with one hand still on her doorknob. She had a small shoe box in her other hand.

Liza froze, too. She couldn't walk with Heather. But Bridget lived in the same direction as Monica Marks. So what could she do?

She could wait for Heather to go first. But then she would have to walk behind Heather all the way to Monica's house.

Or she could start walking now. She could hurry past Heather's house and keep going. But then Heather would be following *her*.

Or she could go back into her own house and let Heather leave—give her a good head start.

No, she thought, I won't do that. I won't hide. And she began to walk.

At the same time, Heather let go of her doorknob and ran down her steps. She turned and started off toward Monica's house. She was ahead of Liza.

Liza just kept going. She felt dumb walking behind Heather as if they were a parade.

Heather turned back for a moment. "Stop following me," she said.

"I'm not following you." Liza was glad she wasn't the first one after all.

Heather speeded up.

So did Liza.

Heather turned back again. "I said *Stop following me*, Liza. And I *mean* it."

"I said *I'm not following you*, Heather. And I *mean* it." Liza knew that she wasn't being very nice. She couldn't stop herself. The faster Heather walked, the faster Liza walked.

Finally Heather began to run. So did Liza, but Heather was a faster runner. She was almost half a block ahead of Liza when she looked back over her shoulder.

Liza saw Heather trip. She saw her fly forward and land on the sidewalk. She heard her cry out.

C H A P T E R

Fourteen

Liza ran up to Heather. "Are you all right?"

Heather sat on the sidewalk. Blood trickled from her scraped knees. She was crying.

Liza tried to help her up.

"Leave me alone!" said Heather. "Just get away from me."

Liza stepped back. "I was only trying to help."

"Liar!" shouted Heather. "You were not. You did it on purpose. Monica was right about you."

Liza's eyes filled with tears. "I didn't know you were going to fall," she said. "I didn't want you to get hurt."

Heather stood up slowly. "Just go away. I'm never going to talk to you again."

But Liza couldn't go away. Heather's knees looked terrible. Liza knew they must hurt a lot. "I'm sorry," she said. "I really am."

Heather pulled a tissue from her pocket. She wiped her tears away. Then she dabbed at her bloody knees.

Liza stood there. She wanted to help. But she didn't know what to do. Then she saw the box that Heather had been carrying. It was lying on the ground, smashed. She picked it up.

"Heather," she said, "you dropped this. I think you fell on it."

Heather looked up. "Oh, no! My cupcakes." She grabbed the box from Liza and pulled the lid off. "They're ruined!" She started crying again.

Liza knew what those cupcakes were for. They were to share with Monica Marks. For a moment, she was glad they got smashed. But then she thought about Heather. "I'm sorry," she said again.

"You're not sorry about anything," cried

Heather. "It's all your fault." She turned and limped away.

Liza caught up with her. "Are you still going to Monica's house? Maybe you should go home first . . . get your knees fixed up."

Heather didn't answer. She just kept walking. She threw the smashed box into a garbage can as she passed.

Liza walked along next to her. "Listen, Heather," she said. "I wasn't following you. Honest."

No answer.

"I was going to Bridget's house."

No answer.

"I still *am* going to Bridget's house, but only for the morning. And I'm not going shopping with my mother this afternoon. I wanted to tell you last night. I tried. But you . . . you know. Oh, come on, Heather. Please don't be mad at me."

No answer. But Heather didn't look quite as angry. She looked as if she was thinking things over.

Liza was thinking, too. And when they got to Monica's house, she knew what she had to do. She held out her bag of cookies. "Here," she said. "You can have these. They're oatmeal cookies."

Heather just looked at the bag for a moment.

Liza was afraid she wasn't going to take it.

"Well," said Heather finally, "it *is* your fault my cupcakes got ruined." She reached out and took the bag from Liza. "Thanks," she mumbled. "I guess I'll see you this afternoon."

Liza smiled. "Okay," she said.

Heather rang Monica's doorbell.

"See you later," said Liza. Then she hurried away. She didn't want to be there when Monica came out.

Fifteen

Liza smiled to herself as she walked to Bridget's house. She was glad she'd given those cookies to Heather. Now everything would be okay.

She was still smiling as she rang Bridget's doorbell.

Bridget opened the door. She was not smiling. "Liza," she said. "I have to tell you something." Then she rushed outside and closed the door behind her.

"What's the matter?" said Liza. "What happened?"

Bridget looked back at her house. "William is here. And so is his mother."

Liza felt her stomach get tight. What if William *had* told his mother on them after all? "Maybe I should go home," she said.

"No!" cried Bridget. "You can't. My mother already told them you were coming. And anyway, they're only here to visit. Really." She opened the door.

Liza just stood there.

"Please," begged Bridget. "I would do it for you."

Liza took a deep breath. She followed Bridget into the house.

"Come on in and sit down, girls," said Bridget's mother.

Liza looked around quickly. They were in the living room—Mrs. Duffy's studio. A big easel stood in one corner. William and his mother were sitting on the couch. They were both dressed up. They were both skinny.

Mrs. Duffy sat on the only chair. The rest of the floor was covered with packing boxes.

Bridget and Liza sat down on two of the boxes.

"Liza," said Bridget's mother, "do you know

Mrs. Spear, our next-door neighbor? And of course you know William from school."

"Hello," said Liza. She smiled politely. She wished she could escape.

Mrs. Spear sat on the edge of her seat, her back straight, her hands folded neatly in her lap. "It's always lovely to meet one of William's friends," she said.

William stared at his knees. His ears were red.

Liza wondered if he had any friends at all. Probably not, she decided.

"We won't stay," said Mrs. Spear. "I can see that we picked a bad time for a visit."

Good, thought Liza.

"Not at all," said Mrs. Duffy. "Let me make some coffee."

Bridget jumped up. "I'll help you, Mom."

"No," said her mother. "You can stay here and talk with our guests."

Bridget sat down again and began to chew on a fingernail.

Liza shot her a dirty look.

"So," said Mrs. Spear. "You three are all in the same class. That's nice, isn't it?"

"Yes," said Liza.

"Yes," said Bridget.

William was still studying his knees. He sniffed.

"Use a tissue, William," said his mother. She took one from her purse and handed it to him.

Poor William, thought Liza. How could his mother embarrass him like that?

Mrs. Duffy came back into the room. "Bridget," she said, "we're out of milk. Would you run to the store, please?"

"I'll go, too," said Liza. She scrambled up. No way was she going to be stuck here alone.

"Fine," said Bridget's mother. "You can buy cookies while you're there. Any kind you like." She handed some money to Bridget. "William, why don't you go with them?"

Liza looked at William. He was slumped down in his seat. *Say no,* she thought. *Please say no.*

"No," said Mrs. Spear. "William can't run. He's got allergies, you know. Just like his father when he was a little boy." She patted William's arm. "You stay here with me."

William looked as if he wanted to die.

Poor, poor William, thought Liza. "We won't run," she said out loud.

Everybody stared at her.

Liza could hardly believe what she was saying. "We'll walk," she went on. "Then William can come with us. Okay?"

"Well," said Mrs. Spear, "I guess that will be all right. As long as you don't run. Go ahead, William."

William didn't look any happier than he had before. But he got up and followed Liza out of the room. "Why did you do that?" he said as soon as they were outside.

Liza shrugged. She didn't want to tell William that she felt sorry for him.

They began to walk. Liza was in the middle. She could *feel* William walking along next to her. And she could hear him—sniff . . . sniff. At first they were little sniffles. Then they got louder. Finally William sneezed.

Liza moved quickly away from him. She bumped into Bridget. They both giggled nervously.

William glared at them. "Why don't you both just leave me alone?" he said in a low, angry voice. "I saw what you did to my picture."

Then he turned his face away from them. He walked on, staring at the sidewalk.

"We didn't mean anything," said Liza. "And I already said I was sorry I took your pictures."

William muttered something.

"Listen, William," said Bridget. "We thought your pictures were good. They were really funny. And we *are* sorry about what we did. Now we just want to be friends. Okay?"

Friends? thought Liza. She didn't want to be friends with William Spear. She just felt sorry for him. She waited to see what William would say.

William didn't answer.

Liza made a face at Bridget, but Bridget didn't seem to notice.

They kept walking until they came to a small corner store. Then they all went inside.

First they got the milk. Then they found the cookies.

"I like soft cookies," said Liza. "Soft and chewy."

"I like chocolate," said Bridget. She picked up a box of chewy chocolate-chip cookies. "These look good. Should we get them?"

"Okay," said Liza.

William scowled. He didn't say anything.

Bridget paid for the cookies and milk. As soon as they were outside, she opened the box. "My mother won't mind," she said. "And I'm starving." She helped herself.

So did Liza.

Bridget held the box out to William, but he shook his head no.

Bridget shrugged and took another cookie for herself.

They started walking again.

Mrs. Duffy was waiting for them. She took some cookies and put them on a plate. Then she offered them to William's mother.

"Thank you," said Mrs. Spear. "These look delicious. But I'm afraid William can't have any. William," she said, "didn't you tell the girls that you're allergic to chocolate?"

Sixteen

That was the worst," Liza said to Bridget. "I didn't think they would ever leave."

"Shhhh. Not so loud," said Bridget. "They might hear you." Her mother was letting Mrs. Spear and William out.

Liza and Bridget waited in the living room.

Liza sat down on the edge of the couch and folded her hands like Mrs. Spear. *"Blow your nose, William. Don't run, William. Chocolate is bad for you, William. . . ."* She groaned and slumped back onto the couch.

Bridget's mother came into the living room. "Okay, girls, let's get to work."

"Mom," said Bridget. "Why is Mrs. Spear

so mean to William? She won't let him do *anything*. And she's always picking on him."

Liza leaned forward. She wanted to hear the answer.

Mrs. Duffy sighed. She sat down on a packing box. "She's not being mean," she said. "She just worries about William."

"But why?" said Bridget.

Her mother stood up again. "William was very sick when he was a baby. But he's okay now. He just has allergies." She looked around the room. "Come on, girls. We've got a lot to do."

The three of them set to work. They worked hard for the rest of the morning.

Finally Mrs. Duffy said, "You two have done enough. Why don't you take a break now? And I'll order a pizza. You deserve it."

"Great!" said Bridget. "Let's go upstairs, Liza."

"I'll call you when the pizza comes," said her mother.

Liza followed Bridget up to her room. She dropped onto the floor.

Bridget went over to her window and looked out. "William's not there," she said. "He must be inside."

Liza made a face. "Your mother says William is okay now. But he doesn't *act* okay. He acts weird."

Bridget sat down on the floor. "You know," she said, "I was thinking. I really feel sorry for William, because of his mother and everything. He's not so bad. And what I was thinking was, maybe we could be his friends or something."

"No," said Liza quickly.

Bridget gave her a look.

Liza didn't want Bridget to think she was a mean, horrible person. "I would do it," she said, "but William probably doesn't want to be friends with us. Ummm . . . because we're girls."

Bridget thought it over for a moment. "I'm going to ask him," she said. "Will you do it with me?"

Liza wanted to say no. She wanted to say that she didn't like William, that she did *not* want to be his friend, that nobody did. But she was afraid Bridget wouldn't like her anymore if she said that. And Bridget was her only friend in Mrs. Rumford's class.

"Will you?" said Bridget again.

"Okay," Liza mumbled. "I'll do it." She crossed her fingers for luck. Maybe Bridget would forget about it. Liza would just die if Heather saw her with William Spear.

"We can ask him Monday morning," said Bridget. "I'll meet you in the schoolyard. Okay?"

Liza gulped. She couldn't do it. Not in front of the whole school. No way.

Bridget was waiting for an answer.

"Girls," called Mrs. Duffy. "Come on down. The pizza's here."

"Let's go," said Liza. "I'm starving." She jumped up and headed for the door. She had to make Bridget forget.

Bridget ran after her.

There was a big white pizza box on the kitchen table.

"Yum," said Liza. "It smells delicious."

They both helped themselves to a slice. "This is the best," said Bridget. "I love it with extra cheese."

Liza just nodded. Her mouth was full of pizza.

Mrs. Duffy came into the room, holding her coffee mug. "Don't forget about your ballet class, Bridget."

"I remember," said Bridget. "Two o'clock."

Mrs. Duffy filled her mug. Then she went back to her studio.

"I didn't know you take ballet classes," said Liza.

Bridget smiled. "Since I was five years old," she said. She stood up and did a little curtsy. Then she sat down and took a big bite of pizza. Some tomato sauce dribbled onto her chin.

Liza tried to imagine Bridget as a ballerina. But it was hard. "Do you like ballet?" she said.

Bridget swallowed. "My old ballet school was pretty good. And my best friend, Kate, was in my class. But I don't know about this place." She frowned a little. "Today is my first time."

Liza took another slice of pizza. She wondered what ballet classes were like. She wondered what this Kate was like, too. There were so many things she didn't know about Bridget. Not like Heather. She and Heather knew everything about each other. They'd been best friends since they were babies.

"Hey," said Bridget. "I have an idea. You can come with me. You can watch my class, and then we can—"

"I can't," said Liza. "I have to go home soon." Heather might be there already.

Bridget looked disappointed.

"Maybe I can come another time," said Liza. "I really want to."

"Okay." Bridget popped her last bite of pizza crust into her mouth. "Do you have to go home right now? Can you stay a little while?"

Liza thought for a moment. She did want to stay a little longer. But what if Heather was waiting for her right now? "I'd better go," she said.

Bridget walked her to the door. "I'll see you Monday."

"See you Monday," Liza repeated. She went outside.

As soon as the door closed, Liza began to walk and to think about Heather. Was Heather still mad about their fight? Did Heather and Monica have a good time at Monica's house? Liza hoped not. She had to find out. She had to talk to Heather.

Liza walked faster and faster. Finally she began to run. She was out of breath when she got to Heather's house. She ran up the steps and leaned on the doorbell.

Heather's mother opened the door. "Hello, Liza," she said. "I'm sorry, but Heather's not home."

Seventeen

Where was Heather?

Liza threw open her front door. *"Mom,"* she yelled. "Did Heather call?"

"Mom's not here," Edward yelled back from the kitchen. He came out with a sandwich in one hand and a banana in the other. A container of juice was tucked under his arm.

Liza could smell the peanut butter as he passed her on his way upstairs. "You're not supposed to eat in your room," she said. "Do you want to get ants?"

"What are you, my mother?" Edward kept going.

"Where *is* Mom?" said Liza.

"She took Peggy to the park." Edward disappeared down the hall. "She took the dog, too." Then his door slammed, and Liza could hear the blast of his rock music.

Liza hated super-loud rock music. She decided to go outside to wait for Heather. She let the door slam on her way out. Edward wouldn't hear it anyway.

Liza looked up the street. No one was coming. She sat down on a step to wait. She hoped that Heather would come soon.

But what if she didn't?

Liza began to worry.

What if Heather *had* told Monica about their fight this morning? Then Monica would say that Liza was a bad friend. Monica would say that Heather should stay at her house all day. And Heather would say, "Okay." And then . . . then they would laugh and eat up all of Liza's chewy oatmeal cookies.

Liza groaned. Of course Heather wasn't coming. Why should she? Monica Marks was

Heather's best friend now. And there wasn't anything she could do about it.

Liza stood up. "I don't care," she said. "I'll show her. She thinks I'll just sit here waiting for her all day. Well, she's wrong." Liza took one last look up the street. Then she went back into her house.

Edward's music floated down from his room. But the rest of the house felt empty. Liza turned the television on—boring. She turned it off again. She went into the kitchen. But she wasn't hungry. She wandered out to the front porch. Her backpack was lying on the floor where she'd dropped it Friday afternoon. Liza gave it a little kick. "Stupid thing," she mumbled.

But the backpack made her think about school—and the math test Monday morning. Bridget was going to study for it. Liza opened the backpack. Maybe she should study, too. She'd learn her number facts so well that everyone would be amazed. She'd be the smartest kid in the whole third grade. Even Heather would hear about it.

Liza started pulling things out of the backpack. She took her yellow reader out and dumped it on the floor. Then she picked it up again. Maybe she should read for a while first. She could work on number facts later.

Yes, that's what she'd do. After all, she needed to work on her reading, too, if she wanted to be the smartest kid in third grade. And she liked to read. She did *not* like number facts.

Liza took her reader outside. She sat down on a step and opened the book. Then she found her place. She was reading a story about a girl who wanted a bicycle. The girl's family had no extra money for things like bikes.

Liza wanted a new bike herself. She read fast to see if the girl in the story would get one.

"Hey, what are you doing?"

Liza blinked. She looked up from her book. *"Heather!"*

Eighteen

Heather had Band-Aids on both of her knees. She sat down next to Liza on the step.

Liza closed her book. "I didn't think you were coming."

"I told you I was only going to Monica's house for the morning," said Heather. "And anyway, Monica's not home this afternoon. Guess where she went."

"Where?" said Liza. She hoped it was far away.

"To her ballet class," said Heather. "I didn't even know she took ballet. Did you?"

"No." Liza wondered if it was the same

ballet class that Bridget was in. It could be. "Bridget takes ballet, too," she said. "I think she's pretty good at it."

Liza and Heather sat quietly for a few minutes.

"You know," said Heather, "it's funny the way everything is turning out this year. You're getting to be friends with Bridget. And I'm getting to be friends with Monica."

Liza looked at Heather's knees. "Did you tell Monica about what happened this morning?" She held her breath, waiting for Heather to say no.

Heather touched one bandaged knee. "Yes," she said. "I did. I was still really mad at you."

"Oh." Liza felt tears coming. She turned her face away.

"But listen," said Heather. "I told her that you were sorry. And I told her that you gave me your cookies."

"You did?"

"Yes," said Heather. "And now I'm not even mad at you."

Liza wiped her eyes. "Let's not fight any-more, Heather. Okay? Not ever again."

"Okay," said Heather. "No more fights." She stood up. "I didn't eat lunch yet. Do you want to come home with me?"

"Sure," said Liza. "But I'm not hungry. I had pizza at Bridget's house."

Heather giggled. "I can see that." She pointed at Liza's shirt.

Liza looked down. There was a big tomato-sauce stain right in the middle of her T-shirt. "Oh, brother," she said. "Bridget didn't even tell me. Wait a minute. I'll go get a clean one."

Liza ran inside and up the stairs to her room. She found a clean T-shirt and changed into it. Then she banged on Edward's door. "Tell Mom I'm going to Heather's house," she shouted. She ran downstairs again.

Heather was waiting for her. She was hold-ing Liza's yellow reader. "Why are you reading this on *Saturday?*" she said.

Liza shrugged. Her plan to be the smartest kid in third grade didn't sound so great now.

It sounded kind of dumb. She opened her porch door and tossed the book onto her backpack. She would finish reading the story later.

Right now she just wanted to go to Heather's house. She wanted to tell Heather all about Bridget. But not about the plan to be friends with William Spear. Heather would think she was crazy.

Liza tried to push the William problem from her mind. "I'm ready," she said to Heather. "Let's go."

Nineteen

It was Monday morning.

Liza and Heather were walking to school. They were wearing jeans and red T-shirts and matching butterfly belts. They were best friends again.

But Liza was worried. She hadn't told Heather about Bridget's plan—the plan to be friends with William Spear. She knew that Heather would *not* understand. *Nobody* would understand!

Liza sighed. Maybe she would be lucky. Maybe Bridget or William would be late or absent. Or maybe Bridget would forget about her dumb plan. That would be the best.

They kept walking until they came to the schoolyard gate.

The yard was already crowded. Liza looked around nervously. She didn't see Bridget or William. But she did see Monica Marks.

Monica was standing with some other kids from Mrs. Lane's class. She waved at Heather. "Over here," she called.

"Let's go," said Heather.

"No." Liza shook her head. "You go. She doesn't mean me."

But Heather grabbed her arm and dragged her over to the group.

"Hi, Heather," said Monica. She moved to make a space for Heather next to her.

Liza wished she hadn't come. These kids used to be her friends. But now all they cared about was Monica Marks.

"Hi, Liza." It was Kelly. She was smiling.

Liza smiled back.

"Liza," said Robin, "it's too bad you got Rumford. It really wasn't fair."

A couple of other kids stopped talking to each other.

Liza couldn't believe it. They were all looking at her.

"What's Rumford like?"

"Is she really that bad?"

"Tell us."

Monica Marks scowled. "Oh, who cares about that?" she said. "Let's talk about something else."

But nobody answered her. They were all waiting for Liza.

"Well," said Liza slowly. "It's true. Mrs. Rumford is the meanest teacher I ever had."

Everyone moved a little closer.

"You wouldn't believe all the work she makes us do and the homework. And if you don't do it, she . . . she even made one kid *cry*. It was terrible."

"It *is* true," said Heather. "Liza was doing homework on *Saturday*. I saw her."

"Big deal," said Monica.

But Liza didn't care what Monica said. She

felt great with all her old friends around her. It was almost like last year.

Then Bridget tapped her on the shoulder.

"Liza," she said. "I just got here. William's over by the wall."

"Who?" said Heather.

Liza couldn't believe it—Bridget was going to ruin everything. "Uh . . . nobody," she said to Heather. She turned toward Bridget. *"Not now,"* she said in a low voice. She wished Bridget would disappear—and take William Spear with her.

First Bridget looked confused, then hurt. Then she turned from Liza and walked away.

Liza bit her lip. She felt terrible, but what could she do? It was Bridget's fault. *She* was the one who wanted to be friends with William. Liza watched her make her way across the yard.

"Who is that girl?" said Kelly. "She's weird."

Liza sighed. "She's new. Her name is Bridget."

"Bridget Duffy," said Monica. "She's in my ballet class." She giggled. "She's really creepy.

Her leotard is too big. It's all baggy. And it's green. Nobody wears green." She made a face. "Isn't she *your* friend, Liza?"

Everybody looked back and forth, from Monica to Liza.

Liza didn't know what to do. She felt like a mouse trapped by a cat.

Monica was smiling now—her mean smile.

Liza stared at her. She stared at that mean smile. She knew what she had to do. "Bridget *is* my friend," she said. "And she's a better friend than you any day." Then she turned her back on her old friends and went to find Bridget.

Monica just laughed as Liza walked away. But Liza didn't care. Monica was not her friend. She never would be.

"Liza," called Heather.

Liza didn't stop. She kept going until she reached Bridget and William. "Um . . . hi," she said to both of them. "Did you study for the math test? I did a little bit."

Bridget looked surprised for a moment, then

happy. "I did," she said. "How about you, William?"

William didn't say anything. His ears turned red.

Liza tried to look friendly. It wasn't easy. But she did it anyway.

Finally William said, "I studied."

A whistle blew three times. "Line up," called the principal.

Everybody started to move. Liza and Bridget and William walked toward their line together.

"Bridget," Liza whispered, "did you ask him about being friends yet?"

"No," said Bridget. "Why?"

"I'll tell you later." Liza had decided something. She would be nice to William. She wouldn't tease him again. But she couldn't ask him to be friends. She hoped Bridget would understand.

They kept walking until Liza felt a tug on her backpack.

It was Heather. Liza stopped.

"Don't be mad," said Heather. "Monica didn't mean anything."

Ha! thought Liza. Monica did *so* mean something. "It's okay," she said. "I'm not mad."

Heather smiled. "Good. Meet me after school?"

"Okay." Liza smiled back. She felt wonderful. Heather was still her best friend.

Heather ran off to join her own class.

Liza caught up with Bridget and William. They were at the end of Mrs. Rumford's line. They were practicing number facts.

A whistle blew. The line started to move.

"Liza," said Bridget. "Are you ready for the math test?"

"Ready," said Liza. She crossed her fingers for good luck. Liza was ready for anything.

Barbara Baker is a former elementary-school teacher and the author of *Third Grade Is Terrible*. Ms. Baker's other books include *Digby and Kate*, *Digby and Kate Again*, *N-O Spells No!* and *Oh, Emma!* She lives in New York City.

Ann Iosa has illustrated books and educational materials for children. She lives in Connecticut.